The Stupid Goose
Copyright © Lars Bo Appel, 2024
All rights reserved
This edition © Wilderness State, 2024
Written and Illustrated by Lars Bo Appel

1st edition, 1st printing 2024
ISBN 978-87-974010-4-0
www.wildernessstate.com

NIETZSCHE
SARTRE
A. LINDGREN
ROUSSEAU
KIERKIGAARD
S.D.BEAUVOIR
CAMUS

Villa Viva Fables
*(inspired by a time that
never should have been)*

1. Fable: About Cooperation.
The Fox that suddenly became
a bit too chubby

2. Fable: About Society.
The Lazy Dog who gave a speech
no-one listened to

3. Fable: About Fear.
The Wolf beneath the star

The Fable of

The Cunning Fox
Who Suddenly Became
a Bit Too Chubby

The Lazy Dog lay there, doing - well, what he liked best. Which, not very surprisingly, was - absolutely nothing. If it hadn't been for an annoying fly, he would have been sweetly asleep. But every time he was about to drop off, he got interrupted. So, one eye was almost always open. The Lazy Dog's head got filled with all the exciting chaotic things happening around Villa Viva. Even though he preferred to do nothing, he couldn't help but wonder. For example, about The Crazy Rooster.

It had been a long time since The Crazy Rooster had made noise and crowed in the morning. Actually, it had been quite nice. Now, everyone was only woken up when The Angry Wife slammed the kitchen window open and shouted as angrily as she could (and she could):

"Get up and get going, you lazy dogs."

Which The Lazy Dog found peculiar. Why should he get up when he was, after all, the Lazy Dog and chained up? What was the use of him getting up? The next thing she did next was to go to The

Dominant Hens. And that was another thing The Lazy Dog found highly mysterious. Lately, The Angry Wife's facial expression had been mild and happy when she stepped out of the henhouse with the basket full of eggs. Sometimes more than once a day. The fact they were overflowing with eggs was suspicious in itself, as The Dominant Hens liked to control everyone else and do as little as possible. Why had they suddenly become so diligent? There had to be something fishy going on.

The Lazy Dog became more and more curious. So, even though he didn't really feel like it, he called The Stupid Goose over to him when she unceremoniously strolled past the doghouse.

"Psst, you Stupid Goose, come here, I need to talk to you."

The Stupid Goose was on the verge of a heart attack, no one in the garden normally bothered to talk to her. At first, she thought it was a mistake and tried to walk away, so he had to call her again. Slowly and uncertainly, she

approached the dangerous but - fortunately - chained dog. As she got close, The Lazy Dog smiled welcomingly, which made her relax. No one usually smiled at her either. In a deep and confidential whisper, The Lazy Dog said to her:

"Do you know where The Crazy Rooster is?"

"No, it puzzles me too."

It blurted out of her beak. Because it was really strange that he was gone. The Crazy Rooster had always been a bit under the thumb in the henhouse, but to run away outright! None of them had expected that.

"I'll take a stroll and ask the other animals in the garden, if they've heard anything. I have time, while The Angry Wife doesn't know my gate is open,"

whispered The Stupid Goose. And true to her word, she did just that. A couple of hours later, she came back and was able to tell that no one else had seen anything. The only one who seemed to know something were The Dominant Hens.

"I asked every single one. Every time they tried to
say something, The Most Dominant Hen
cleared her throat. This made each hen either
shut their beaks or change their explanation.
When I got to The Most Dominant Hen, she
simply said - 'Your time is up, you Stupid Goose.
We have meetings scheduled. So if you would
be so kind as to leave our henhouse.' See, that's
strange, isn't it?"

concluded The Stupid Goose. The Lazy Dog
nodded - yes, one could certainly say that.
The whole thing remained a bit of a mystery.
That is, until the next day when the mystery got
even bigger. The Lazy Dog lay as usual,
dreaming. Today, he was dreaming that a giant
meat bone was gently knocking because it wanted
to come into his doghouse. It knocked a little less
gently and more forcefully the third time. In the
dream, The Lazy Dog said:

" Just come on in, even though I'm not
particularly fond of meat bones."

He woke up with a startled jolt at the sound of his own voice. The shock didn't diminish when the meat bone responded:

"Alright I'm coming in."

"Am I still dreaming, or what?"

stammered The Lazy Dog. But he wasn't dreaming. Because the meat bone peeked around the corner of the doghouse. It turned out to be a strangely large and disheveled hen who, with a deep meat bone voice, said:

"Hey."

"Who are y-y-you?"

Which was the only sensible thing The Lazy Dog could come up with.

"It's just me - The Crazy Rooster."

"What - how - you don't look like The Crazy Rooster at all."

"No I've disguised myself to get some peace and quiet."

"Get peace and quiet from whom?"

"From The Dominant Hens, of course. By disguising myself as a hen, they let me go about my own business."

Now The Lazy Dog could see that it was indeed The Crazy Rooster, adorned with discarded white feathers. They sat somewhat awkwardly on his body, tied in place with strings. In addition, he had used beak-stick and concealed his comb under a bonnet. The Crazy Rooster continued:

"It's completely crazy in the hen house. They've been holding meetings for weeks now, trying, as they say, to find a more fair distribution of resources. That's why I had to stop crowing so they could have peace and be well-rested for the daily meeting activities."
The Lazy Dog was on the verge of saying:

"Actually a good idea if The Crazy Rooster could

keep quiet.”

But he kept it to himself. The Crazy Rooster continued:

”Next they’ve made a long list of things that are
prohibited in the henhouse. However, the rules
only apply to those who don’t lay eggs. Which
means me.”

The Cracy Rooster sighed and looked down at the
ground in resignation.

”But don’t you think you’ve gone too far? Given
in too much to their pressure?”

asked The Lazy Dog.

”Yeah maybe, but you can’t fight all the time,”

One might have to, or else they’ll never stop The
Lazy Dog thought for him self - but instead, he said:
”Yes you might be right about that,”

“Well you see,”

began The Crazy Rooster.

"The problem is, it just keeps getting worse, and they're completely unstoppable. First, there was just one point on the list. You know that one, I had to stop crowing. So I thought, okay, that's fine, I'll stop for peace's sake. But it just didn't go as expected. Every time I've accepted one point, another one comes up. Now there are 127. At last, in the end, I decided to go into disguise, so I look like them - so far, they've been fine with that."

The Lazy Dog shook his head and sighed. While listening to The Crazy Roosters complaints.

"But the list of things I'm not allowed to do is just the beginning. The Dominant Hens are tired of being stuck in a treadmill or hamster wheel, as they say. So, they've come up with an idea."
"Tell me, what's the idea?"

exclaimed The Lazy Dog. This conversation was finally getting a bit exciting.

"I simply don't know. The day they were getting

close to a solution, they asked me to step outside the hen house. So I did. And it turned out to be the best thing I could have done. Firstly I got away from their idea, and those kind of ideas usually mean trouble for me. And secondly, I suddenly felt free.”

”Why are you still dressed up as a hen, then?”

The Lazy Dog wanted to know.

”Now I’ve become used to it. And I just don’t want to mess with the current state of affairs. As long as I look like a hen, it’s as if they leave me alone. Now I have my daily life around in various gardens, where I have made new friends with whom I play cards and read books. It’s a bit like what I heard The Stupid Goose say the other day when she quoted the philosopher Socrates: To be yourself, you must ask yourself what it is you want - cause no one else can do that for you. And that’s exactly what I’ve started to do.”

“Yeah really?”

thought The Lazy Dog. He was about to say something about the ideas from the hen house sounding like a bad omen. But he was interrupted before the thought turned into words.

The sound of tires on gravel from the driveway made everyone look up. What now? Was Villa Viva expecting guests? Who could it be? Even The Dominant Hens stopped their clucking. The Lazy Dog and The Crazy Rooster halted their conversation. Mostly because the rooster ran away so quickly that his borrowed feathers hung behind him like a small white cloud.

”What's wrong with him?”

muttered The Lazy Dog.

”That's maybe why he's called The CRAZY Rooster,”
he said aloud, chuckling a bit.

"What's so funny?"

asked The Stupid Goose. And continued

"You should focus on who is coming to visit - it might be dangerous."

"Welcome,"

almost shouted The Angry Wife, sounding oddly friendly, gentle, and sweet.

"Thank you, thank you. Thanks for the welcome,"

said the two strangers. They had just arrived in a small white car with a sign on the side that read Association of Free-Range Organic Chicken Feet.

"We're here, as we told you on the phone, to inspect your hen house. Never have we heard of a small flock of hens laying so many eggs. It's so many that one would think you're exaggerating - quite a lot. We need to see it with our own eyes"

The Angry Wife proudly showed off the henhouse to the two new arrivals, who turned out

to be hen house judges. Every year they awarded a very much coveted prize to the very very finest and most egg-laying hen house in the country. They looked and felt and wrote down, and sometimes up. An ”uhh” was replaced with an ”oh” and finally a long ”wauuuuw.” All the hens were laying on stacks of eggs. The Angry Wife filled her basket for the third time that day. They bowed reverently before The Angry Wife and solemnly said:

”This is the most amazing hen house we’ve ever seen.”

All the hens were nearly bursting with pride.

”Truly a well-deserved day,”

one could hear The Most Dominant Hen whisper to a fellow hen in their secret language - Cluckish. That way, only the hens themselves understood what she was saying.

And that’s how Villa Viva’s henhouse received the most prestigious prize. The two judges hung a fine certificate on the wall of the henhouse. Unlike Villa Viva's henhouse, the other henhouses in the area had experienced a slight decline in production. So, it was not without a bit of envy and astonishment that the other Angry Wives in the small commuter community later received the news.

Behind the henhouse, The Cunning Fox had been watching everything through a crack in the wall. If anyone had seen him, they would have been able to see that he looked exceptionally proud. After enjoying the performance, he stealthily crept away with his empty sack over his shoulder. He slipped somewhat awkwardly under a hole in the fence and ran up the path to the big tree with the bench. Just as he had the chance to disappear behind the tree and get away, he looked over his shoulder and met the gaze of The Lazy Dog. Even though the dog, the doghouse and the chain were now quite a distance away, there was no doubt. The Lazy Dog had seen him and was about to say:

"Hasn't The Cunning Fox gotten a bit chubby?"

When The Stupid Goose beat him to it and exclaimed loudly:

"Tell me, hasn't The Cunning Fox gotten a bit chubby?"

"Exactly what I was just thinking,"

said The Lazy Dog, looking up:

"Have you been standing behind my doghouse the whole time?"

"Yep."

"Did you hear my conversation with The Crazy Rooster?"
"Yep, and now I think I know why he's called The Crazy Rooster."

"Uh yeah, so?"

"It's not because he crows, because he doesn't."

Started The Stupid Goose and continued:

"It's not because - uh, well, maybe that too."

"What, what?"

The Lazy Dog asked eagerly.

"Yeah, that he's crazy."

"Well"

thought The Lazy Dog, that might also be true.

"But,"

The Stupid Goose continued:

"I think it's more because he's off, just giving up
and giving in to The Dominant Hens. That's weak
and, most importantly, crazy,"
The Lazy Dog endorsed that view. After which he
asked,

"chubby - wonder why?"
The Stupid Goose responded by shrugging. Yes, it
was truly mysterious.

A fox that had suddenly become chubby.
Overproduction of eggs. The Angry Wife, who
was happy. A rooster disguised as a hen. The list
of mysterious things just got longer and longer.
Something had to be done. But what?

The next day, part of the answer came on its own.
Two of The Dominant Hens sat comfortably on
the bench under the big tree and chatted.
As usual, it sounded like a bunch of gibberish.
Only the trained ear could make sense of it.
The Stupid Goose had such an ear.

"Smart - cluck cluck cluck - relax we can now
cluck yes cluck cluck - can we cluck now. Cluck -
a very good deal"

They clucked and cackled away, in Cluckish, their
secret language. The Stupid Goose sat
completely still on the other side of the tree and
noted everything she heard. One of The
Dominant Hens had become so caught up in her
own flow of speech that she eagerly hopped down
from the bench and started walking around.
She clucked and squawked, flapping her wings,

all while the other Dominant Hen nodded and clucked along. Soon, she was heading towards the other side of the tree. Just as The Dominant Hen took a turn around the tree, The Stupid Goose lifted her eyes from the notepad. She managed to move away just in time before being discovered. The only reason she wasn't seen was that the hen had her beak high in the sky while clucking with closed eyes. She pompously uttered some nonsense that came out amid clucks and squawks. It seemed to revolve around the idea that everyone here in Villa Viva, perhaps in the entire country, and almost in the whole world, was completely inferior to The Dominant Hens. The Stupid Goose couldn't help but chuckle silently as she stood behind a bush, watching the two flap their wings and wiggle their tails. They had become so loud that The Most Dominant Hen was on her way up the path. She had to put a damper on their afternoon chatter.

That evening, The Lazy Dog retrieved an alarm clock from the shelf inside his doghouse. He wasn't used to using alarm clocks - he almost hated them. The clock he now held was one of his early inventions. It was divided into different wake-up zones. From 3-4 in the morning, it said: "Oh, for heaven's sake, I absolutely don't want to be disturbed". From 4-5 in the morning, it was written: "It's way too early," and from 5-6: "Tell me, what's going on? Can't you see what time it is?". From 6 in the morning until 4 the next morning, it said: "Shhhhh, I don't want to be disturbed." During that period, the clock couldn't be made to work at all. The Lazy Dog set the clock to wake up at - "It's way too early." He placed the clock aside and lay down, closed his eyes, while thinking about what The Stupid Goose had told him. It was sure to be fun.

At 'way too early,' the clock began its clever waking ritual. A feather was slowly lowered from the ceiling. The feather approached The Lazy Dog's nose. And the moment it touched the nose, it stopped. Now it began to sway from side to side. The Lazy Dog started to move. He tried to swipe the feather away from his nose with his paw. But there was a clever electronic eye that moved around and ensured that the feather moved in just the right way. The moment the paw would swipe at the feather, "the little eye" made sure the feather was lifted up. Immediately after, it was back on the nose, and this went on for a while until The Lazy Dog, annoyed, opened one eye.

" Oh no - it's way too early,"

The Lazy Dog muttered hoarsely, and that was true enough, for that's what he had asked for. The Lazy Dog opened his eyes. At that moment, the eye and the feather disappeared. He had developed this wake-up gadget so he could be awakened without disturbing others. He stretched and was about to go back to sleep when he remembered what he had to do now.
A broad and somewhat sinister smile spread across his lips, revealing his large and dangerous teeth shining white in the moonlight. Now was the time. Let's see if the Dominant Hens were as smart as they claimed to be.
He retrieved his secret key from the shelf. No one knew that he had a copy of the key to the padlock that his collar was chained to. It gave him a delightful freedom, which he used when no one

saw it. Like now, when everyone was asleep.
It was a dangerous time of day, though, as it
wouldn't be long before the house woke up.
But The Silly Goose had told him that this was
the time everything would happen. He really
wanted to see it with his own eyes. He whispered
eagerly to himself:

"Imagine if that story is really true. Pretty wild."

Now that he had freed himself from the chain, he
could cautiously sneak across the dark courtyard,
heading towards the henhouse. All was quiet and
peaceful. He peered gently through a crack

between two boards. All the Dominant Hens
were snoring away. But it didn't take long before
the sound of paws tiptoeing over cobblestones
filled the darkness. A shadow glided across the
courtyard and into the henhouse. Everything was
unfolding just as The Stupid Goose had said. One
might think that all the Dominant Hens would
spring up now that a stranger was sneaking into
their domain. But nothing happened. The Lazy
Dog observed that The Goose's account had held
true up until now. He cautiously emerged from
his hiding place and tried to step unnoticed into
the henhouse. However, as soon as he stepped on
the first floorboard, the floor gave way under his
weight. There was a loud creak. The Dominant
Hen jolted awake and turned on the light. All the
other Dominant Hens woke up with a squawk.
Another squawk erupted as they saw The Lazy
Dog looming in the doorway, creating a flurry of
white feathers as they fluttered around in
confusion. Out of the feather cloud came words
and shouts:
"What, how, why, and especially where - is - your
- chain?"

They all shouted at each other. The Most Dominant Hen called the flock to order and asked.

"Hey tell me, what in the name of the henhouse are you doing here?"

While the last feather drifted down and settled on the ground, The Lazy Dog spoke with his deepest and most serious voice:

"I just wanted to see if I could lay eggs - like the fox." The Lazy Dog pointed at The Cunning Fox, who stood at the back of the henhouse. The fox was completely still, as if it were petrified. One hand held a chicken, while the other was in the process of placing an egg under it. Now, standing there completely still in the light from the bulb in the ceiling, it was clear to see that The Cunning Fox had become a bit plump. That was also the reason why he didn't run away. He simply couldn't. The hole in the back wall that it used to escape had become too small, and the dog was blocking the doorway. Next to The Cunning Fox was a large sack filled with eggs.

"Yes yes, it might indeed look a bit mysterious,"

tried The Most Dominant Hen, and continued:

"But there is a completely natural explanation."

The Lazy Dog snickered:

"It does seem almost unnatural for a fox to lay eggs,"

With a solemn and assumed authoritative voice, The Most Dominant Hen explained:

"We have thus developed a new distribution key agreement to improve the overall Egg-Production-Capacity-Effect-Enhancement-Digestion-Pleasure with the other henhouses in the area. In collaboration with..."

She hesitated for a moment. Then she almost mumbled in a sort of apologetic cough:

"HrmmpFOX hmpfr."

"What are you saying?"

The dog asked

"I'm saying AND THE FOX FOR CLUCK'S
SAKE."

"Yes I understand that, but what is a distribution
thingamajig?"

The Lazy Dog suddenly looked like someone who
had just received a text message from the moon.
The Stupid Goose had told him most of it, but
that distribution thingamajig was new.

"Ok,"

began the hen condescendingly.

"The Cunning Fox gathers the eggs from all the
henhouse in town - before The Angry Wives come
to collect them. Then he brings the eggs to us.
Here, we distribute all the eggs fairly and take
them back to the henhouses according to our
distribution thingamajig, as you call it."

She spoke very - slowly - and - clearly as one does
to someone who is a bit behind.

"In this way, everyone can get more. Now, that
is truly clever. The Cunning Fox receives eggs
as payment. This way, he serves a purpose and
doesn't need to fight for access to the henhouse.
Everyone welcomes him warmly."

"Aha,"

The Lazy Dog thought.

"That's why he has become chubby. He no longer
has to fight for his prey."

The Most Dominant Hen continued:

"and it earns respect from the Angry Wives, or at
least from our Angry Wife. That is if she knew"
The Cunning Fox let out a long sigh as he
lowered his arms, leaving the egg under the hen.
He hadn't dared to move as long as the Most
Dominant Hen had been speaking. But now,
since she seemed to be finished, and especially

when the topic was about what each house gained from the distribution thingamajig, he felt a bit awkward. The Most Dominant Hen noticed his reaction and glared at him. She cleared her throat unnaturally loudly, signaling to him to keep quiet. The Cunning Fox immediately understood the hint and attempted a bow and a smile. However, he couldn't quite dispel the thick atmosphere that something might be amiss. The Most Dominant Hen on the other hand wondered about the Lazy Dog's reaction. He just stood there without expressing anything. Considering what a wild idea it was, a bit of surprise was the least one could expect. But he didn't flinch. The Lazy Dog now walked right into the center of the hen house. Then he said, as if he had read the thoughts of the Most Dominant Hen:

"Why do you think I'm here right now? It's to catch you in the act"
He rose even further, and his shadow became long, dark, and menacing. Then he glanced over at the Cunning Fox, who at that moment didn't feel particularly cunning.

"Now it's time for you to learn a lesson,"

roared the dog.

"Sssshh,"

said The Most Dominant Hen,

"you're waking everyone up. Just think for a
moment."
She jumped down from her perch and hurried
between the terrified fox and the dog.

"It's silly to ruin what we have. The Angry Wife
is happy. We hens produce less and get praised
for more. The fox has a steady job with a steady
income. Now we just need you to benefit from it
too."

The Lazy Dog, standing there large and
threatening, was completely taken aback by her
words.

"Benefit from it - me?"

He began to calm down a bit because it was nice
that the wife was happy. But he hadn't considered
that he could be a part of the operation.

"How exactly can I benefit from it?"

he asked hesitantly. All The Dominant Hens
stretched their necks and completely stopped
talking in cluckish. Anxiously awaited the
answer.
"The sun is about to rise, and then The Angry
Wife will come, even though she's not so angry at
the moment - thanks to me."
A couple of the Dominant Hens coughed a bit,
prompting the Most Dominant Hen to straighten
herself:

"Uh I mean, of course, thanks to - us."

"So how about you chase The Cunning Fox out
of the chicken coop the moment The Angry Wife
turns on the light? Then she'll perceive you as
a hero, and we can continue our work. Or NOT
work, if you prefer. But we can continue what
we're up to,"

The Most Dominant Hen explained:

"and you'll get better conditions than the ones you already have,"

she added. The Lazy Dog was aware that a decision had to be made now.

"I get to be left alone and can be lazy as usual. The angry wife will look at me with slightly gentler eyes,"

he mumbled to himself.

"What the cluck are you saying?"

clucked The Most Dominant Hen.

"What are you mumbling about? What do you say to the proposal?"

"Uh I say okay,"

stammered the lazy dog. Now they had to move fast before The Angry Wife got up and went into the kitchen. The fox first ran up to the bench and tree, hiding all the distribution eggs. Immediately after, he came back as agreed. Now everything was ready for The Lazy Dog to chase him away. And the moment The Angry Wife turned on the light, the fox ran to the door of the hen house. The Lazy Dog lay in his doghouse as agreed. However, he had almost forgotten what they had agreed upon. So The Most Dominant Hen had to run across the yard and kick him in the butt. That got him up immediately. The noise from the yard made The Angry Wife kick the kitchen door open. Through feathers and chicken commotion, she saw The Cunning Fox standing in the door of the henhouse.

"Hasn't it become a bit chubby?"

she managed to think before she shouted as angrily as she could:

"Get that fox ouuuuut of here."

To her great and delightful surprise, she saw The Lazy Dog on his way to the hen house. The

Cunning Fox ran as fast as he could toward the tree with the bench. That is, as fast as The Lazy Dog could exactly keep up with. On the other side of the tree, they both stopped. Now they just needed the final detail in their play. From the kitchen door, The Angry Wife could no longer see them, but she could hear The Lazy Dog roaring in anger and The Cunning Fox howling in fear. "That will teach the fox a lesson."

She said aloud to herself. The Lazy Dog and The Cunning Fox on the other hand, shook hands to say goodbye. The Cunning Fox disappeared into the large garden. Everything had gone according to plan. "You're soooo gooood, good good lovely sweet nice dog,"

said the Angry Wife as he strutted proudly down towards the chicken menagerie. It was the first time The Lazy Dog had heard her praise him. Normally, she was a bit afraid of him, something she couldn't hide behind her anger. Today, she wasn't angry, but she was still afraid of him. As he approached the kitchen door, she took a step backward onto the first step, then the next step,

until she was inside the kitchen and had closed
the lower part of the half-door. Now she shouted
to The Muted Man:

"you forgot to put the dog on its leash"

A split second later, he stood in the half-door
with her.

"Now go and get that dog chained again"

she ordered.
The Muted Man went outside, thinking:

"As if I enjoy dealing with that dog. I'm not
entirely comfortable with him either,"

The Lazy Dog had lain back in his doghouse. The
Muted Man approached cautiously.
"But what is this now?"

He nearly said out loud but muttered to himself
so no one could hear.

"The chain is back on, how is that possible?

Either the dog wasn't loose, which means my
Angry Wife has just had visions - and I
certainly dare not suggest that. Or the dog has put
the chain on himself, which is completely crazy."
He decided to remain silent, which was, after all,
what he was best at. Additionally, he pretended
as if he had put the chain on.

The Angry Wife became very mild and happy
for a while. She praised The Muted Man, whom
she called - My Brave Man for a short period.
The Lazy Dog was spoiled with meat bones and
compliments. The Dominant Hens and the fox
continued their business for a while. However, it
didn't take long before the other henhouses got
tired of The Dominant Hens and their
distribution contraption. The fox lost weight, the
wife returned to her angry self and The Lazy Dog
was spared meat bones, which for some reason
were not his favourite, anyway.
Uncontrolled and good old-fashioned chaos
fortunately prevailed again in Villa Viva.

The Fable of

The Lazy Dog
who gave a speech
no one listened to

The Lazy Dog lay, as usual, dozing the day away in his doghouse. Perhaps, to his defence, it should be mentioned that a chain prevented him from being able to do much else. However, during the night, he studied, read books, and worked on various ideas for exciting inventions. So, in reality, the Lazy Dog wasn't as lazy as he appeared to be.
He certainly didn't mind doing a little bit, as long as it wasn't something others asked him to do. Therefore, he lay in his chain all day, maintaining an image of being somewhat dangerous and, most importantly, lazy. A good combination if he were to say so himself. This way, he avoided being set in motion to do anything. In the stillness and quiet of the night, however, the Lazy Dog enjoyed his freedom to work on some of his own things. This night, however, was an exception. It started as it usually did. The Angry Wife went into the hen house as the sun went down. She turned off the light and said goodnight.

" She never says goodnight to me,"

sighed the Lazy Dog, and he concluded:

"But here, of course, there's only a faint pale light from my small fridge, which she probably doesn't even know about. On top of that, she's really afraid of me. It is probably just as well that she doesn't pop in to say goodnight to me."

The Dominant Hens used to cluck and squawk until their light was turned off. And, for the most part, they did the same this evening. He waited a bit to make sure that calm had settled in the house and garden. Afterward, he took out his little secret key from the shelf in his doghouse, unlocked the chain, and brought out his Lazy Dog teddy, which he secured to the chain.

"Now no one can see that I'm slipping away,"

He said, glancing out at the yard one last time to make sure it was peaceful and safe. If anyone had been there, they would have seen two identical dogs squeezed together in the entrance of an old doghouse. The upper one looked around a bit strained, with his head pressed against the

ceiling, and the lower one lay as if he really enjoyed it, even though the upper dog's elbow was digging into his forehead.

"All right, now I can get started,"

Whispered The Lazy Dog, the one without a chain, to himself, turning around, and disappeared into the doghouse.

"While the garden slumbers, I will draw my lucky numbers"

He hummed on his way towards the back wall with the small refrigerator with a glass door and the faint, pale light. Next to the refrigerator was the staircase leading down to his secret library, laboratories, and workshops. It was now so quiet that a couple of small cautious clicks sounded like gunshots. At that very moment, the pale light from the refrigerator on the floor mixed with another pale light streaming into the doghouse.

" What on earth is that disturbance?"

exclaimed The Lazy Dog. But no sooner were
the words spoken, a low, hoarse, but penetrating
clucking and cackling started from the other side
of the courtyard. Exactly where the sound had
come from. The sound of the switches turning on
the light in the henhouse.

"But why can't I have peace?"

muttered The Lazy Dog grumpily as he moved
back towards the exit of the doghouse.

"Hua ha ha thihiiii uha ha ha for ten trillion
meat bones"

he shouted out loud while he crawled over The
Lazy Dog teddy's furry body. All the hairs
tickled his belly. So he couldn't help but laugh.
The clucking stopped immediately, and he had
to shove a paw into his mouth to stop his noise. A faint light appeared in the kitchen. It was
The Angry Wife, who had turned on the light in
the bedroom. It became completely silent in the
chicken yard, and the light went out the
moment The Angry Wife turned on the light in

the kitchen. The kitchen door swung open with an angry jerk.

"Tell me, does anyone here know the time? Because my watch must be completely wrong,"

she roared angrily into the darkness. It gave The Lazy Dog a chance to retreat back into the doghouse. As he dragged himself over the furry teddy beneath him, another suppressed sound escaped him. A kind of mixture between a laugh and a scream. Fortunately, she didn't hear it, as she was too busy making a racket herself.

Later in the library, The Lazy Dog tried to concentrate on studying behaviour theory. He had long wondered why people change when they are in a group. His interest in the subject began when The Stupid Goose quoted a philosopher named Nietzsche, who said that insanity among individuals is rare, but in groups, it is quite common. It was in connection with The Dominant Hens bullying her when she spoke the truth. They would just start shouting in her face:

"Stupid stupid stupid goose, stupid stupid dumb dumb."

This, by the way, as how she got her nickname.

The Lazy Dog sat there in his study, immersing himself in the topic but had to give up. The Dominant Hens and their clucking and squawking continued to invade his thoughts. And he kept wondering why they had turned on the light again?

"I wonder what they have been up to?"

On his way up the stairs, it became more evident that the Dominant Hens had resumed their conversation. A hoarse whisper met him. He didn't understand a word of their clucking and squawking. Except for a single word that wasn't in cluckish: Manifesto. He wondered what they needed such a thing for. He put on the chain and took out his mobile phone. He searched for the word - manifesto:

"Aha, it's a kind of declaration of some new rules

for living,"

He thought, putting the phone away before settling down to sleep.

The next morning, the Lazy Dog caught up with The Stupid Goose. Every day, the Angry Wife forgot to close the gate to the goose. So while the Angry Wife collected eggs, the two could easily have a little chat. And that's precisely what they did today. The Lazy Dog tried to reproduce what he had heard from the Dominant Hens in cluck-ish, the best that he could. The Stupid Goose looked at the dog skeptically.

"What are you saying?"

She asked.

"How on earth should I know?"

The dog replied.

"Well, of course. But if you pronounce their clucks even half as well as a beginner, then they're up to something really bad,"

"How bad?"

"On a scale from one to ten, I would say eleven."

Remarked The Stupid Goose..

"That sounds fairly serious."

Acknowledged the Lazy Dog, and continued:

"How can we ensure that we understand their plan?"

"Let me listen to them. Have you recorded any of their clucking?"

The Stupid Goose took it for granted that the Lazy Dog had some technology that could provide them with an answer.

"I don't think I have. But then again, maybe, if I connect the Transponator to the Net-Complicator, then maybe."

They didn't need to find any recordings. Just as they were discussing it, the Most Dominant Hen marched out into the middle of the courtyard. This time she didn't talk in Cluckish. She used their collective language, one that even humans could understand.

"At 12 o'cluck, clucking I mean clock as in o'clock. I will declare a new way for us to interegg ah uh I mean interact,"

She said, looking around angrily, as if it was someone else's fault that she couldn't get her message across. The Lazy Dog and the Stupid Goose looked at each other and said softly in unison:

"At 12 o'clock, we will have it all served."

Precisely on time, all the Dominant Hens marched out of the hen house. In front was the Most Dominant Hen, behind her, the other Dominant Hens followed in a long line, with their beaks held high. At the back was The Crazy Rooster, as usual, dressed as a hen. He still found

it best to submit to avoid trouble. The others in the yard were more uncertain about what he achieved by that choice - to put it mildly.

The Most Dominant Hen positioned herself in the middle of the courtyard. Behind her, all the other hens and the rooster, stood in rows like a military parade. Their clucking and squawking sounded like trumpets as they stomped the ground in rhythm. The Most Dominant Hen stood with her head solemnly bowed forward.

"It seems somewhat drawn-out and quite convoluted."

The Stupid Goose whispered.

"You mean cluckvoluted - he he,"

The Lazy Dog laughed back. The Most Dominant Hen noticed their conversation and barely concealed mockery. Though annoyed she straightened up and raised one wing in the air. Trumpets and stomping ceased instantly.

"IT HAS GONE ON FOR TOO LONG,"

began the Most Dominant Hen, almost shouting:

"ALL TOO LONG."

Once she had everyone's attention, she continued in a threateningly low tone, almost whispering.

"We have carried the heavy load here in the yard."

She looked around to make sure she still got full attention:

"It is us who make things work. Now we have decided that we will enjoy the fruits of our own efforts. From today on, we will establish a pure and democratic society. In the future, we will be the role model that everyone in the whole world will know for,"

She raised her voice

"DEMOCRACY - FREEDOM & UNITY, and

above all,"

There was a suppressed giggle from The Lazy Dog and The Stupid Goose. It was the worst nonsense they had heard in a long time. The interruption made the Most Dominant Hen shout:

"Uh, yeah, yeah, mock away, just cluck yourselves."

She cleared her throat and solemnly looked up into the air, reciting the manifesto they had worked on all night. Everyone watched in astonishment.

"This is a society experiment, cluck cluck."

When she switched to cluckish, it was because she was a bit nervous herself. Everything might have been a bit more apparent in the intense darkness of the night, than now in the midday sun.

"From today, no cluck - uh, no one is allowed to enter the henhouse. And..."

She was interrupted by a car driving into the
courtyard.

"For cluckness' sake. Let me cluck in peace."

Exploded The Most Dominant Hen in rage.
The Angry Wife and The Mutted Man stepped
out of his little white Volkswagen Polo, the one
the wife teasingly called his mini golf. It was a
way to cover up her embarrassment. Because
they didn't drive a fancier car. That they didn't
live on a real farm, or perhaps, more
appropriately on an estate, or in a castle.
The Angry Wife had heard the outburst of the
Most Dominant Hen and now saw the parade in
the courtyard, and shouted out:

"What's going on?"

Before she could get really angry, the Stupid
Goose pulled her aside and quickly explained
what was going on:

"There's absolutely no way that can be
happening."

The Angry Wife exclaimed. But the Most
Dominant Hen stepped forward proudly. All the
Dominant Hens and the Crazy Rooster lined
up like a regiment of soldiers. The Angry Wife
stopped in surprise at their discipline, giving the
Most Dominant Hen the chance to continue:

"YES, I mean, can't one get peace to make
ordinary EGGOLT? CLUCK, I mean, REVOLT for
cluckers. What we have all decided is that from
now on and after that - we call ourselves The
Giant Democratic Roosisters. According to our
manifesto, we will create the most perfect society.
Here everything will be pure and free, because we
ensure that only the chosen ones are allowed in.
On the other hand, there will be no reason to go
out either. All the chosen cluckers will be, well,
cluck-selected. Live freely, cluck cluck. We will
build the perfect and finest social order, where
there is room for all - the right ones."

The Stupid Goose tried to point out that the
abbreviation of their name, GDR, was the same
as a country that once had a failed social model.
A model that could indeed resemble what they

claimed they wanted. She was interrupted by The Giant Democratic Roosisters, shouting in unison:

"STUPID STUPID STUPID GOOSE, CLUCK CLUCK DUMB DUMB."

The Most Giant Democratic Roosister grabbed a list that said SELECTED. She began calling everyone out one by one. Each one called out proudly entered the henhouse. As expected, only hens were called. Even the Crazy Rooster stood bewildered:

"What about me?"

He asked

"Yes what about you?"

Came the cold reply from The Most Giant Democratic Roosister.

"Well, why can't I join?"

She tilted her head, as if to express pity:

"You don't lay eggs - do you?"

He had to admit, of course, that she had a point.

"Oh, well, of course,"

came the apologetic response from him.

"What about The Cunning Fox ?"

shouted The Lazy Dog.

"Yes what about him?"

"He lays eggs, doesn't he?"

the Lazy Dog said laughing, reminding them of
the time when the fox stole from the other
hen houses and laid them under The Dominant
Hens. That way, it seemed like they were laying
more eggs than they actually did.

"I can't remember, cluck, anything cluck about
that. We better get started, cluck, with our new
society,"

Said The Most Giant Democratic Roosister, turning on her heel and marching indignantly into the henhouse. The other chickens followed suit. Two of the now Giant Democratic Roosisters stood guard at the door. A new era had evidently begun. The Muted Man still stood like a statue by his Mini Golf, observing this entire commotion. He said silently to himself:

"Why isn't the Angry Wife selected too? It would make so much sense... to me at least."

A rare smile appeared timidly on the pale man.

"What are you laughing at?"

The Angry Wife grabbed The Muted Man and pulled him away.

"Now I'm going to show you 'funny'. It's the whole house and it must be perfectly clean. Before you serve dinner - on time. Off you go."

That's how it happened that the henhouse was cordoned off from the rest of the garden. At first,

they simply took turns standing guard while some of the other Giant Democratic Roosisters worked on closing the gaps in the fence.
Before the day was over, all the hens were inside the henhouse. As the final touch, the door was blocked with boards. Now it was completely closed.

The next day started as usual. The Angry Wife lit the kitchen light. The Lazy Dog had been looking forward to this moment. He had even set his Feather-source-silent-alarm clock for a time that was way too early. He wouldn't miss this for anything.. The kitchen door opened, and the Angry Wife came out with her basket, heading towards the chicken house. She was only halfway there when a loud voice met her. It wasn't just loud. It was authoritative, or at least commanding. One might be tempted to say, more dominant than democratic.

"Who's there?"

The Angry Wife stopped and looked at a hen peering out through a crack in the door, which had been nailed shut with boards. No one could get out, and no one in. In fact, The Giant Democratic Roosisters didn't want anyone within 6 meters of the chicken house. Now it dawned on the Angry Wife that what she experienced yesterday, which she had perceived as a bad joke, was indeed real.

"Tell me, who do you think you are?"

"The Giant Democratic Roosisters,"

Came the prompt response. The Angry Wife was about to explode. She turned on her heel and slammed the kitchen door behind her.

"What am I going to do?"

She asked The Muted Man without waiting for an answer. Because there never was one anyway.

"You could ask The Angry Neighbour Wife if she has extra eggs,"

The Muted Man's words left her completely

stunned. It actually made sense. The neighbour's
chickens was pretty productive.

"Actually, a good idea,"

she mumbled, as if it were an idea, she had come
up with herself. The Muted Man thought to him
self:

"Now that she unfortunately wasn't chosen, it
would at least be nice if she went in to The Angry
Neighbour Wife. That will give me peace and
quiet for a few hours. Just what I need on my day
off."

The Angry Neighbour Wife indeed had extra
eggs. Payment was - blackberry jam. The Angry
Wife had plenty to spare, after last year's succes-
sful harvest. And it was the same with blackberry
jam as with anything else. If you had too much,
you got tired of it. So, in essence, a really good
deal, especially considering that this year's
harvest seemed to be just as good.

The normal atmosphere in the kitchen almost

became pleasant, and it had an impact on the Angry Wife's mood. It could be felt throughout the garden. In fact, the change was so significant that some started to get quite nervous. The Stupid Goose, as usual, had a comment.

"I agree with Mark Twain, who once said - 'Nothing needs more change than other people's habits'. - BUT this is close to being too much. An angry wife who is happy."

The Lazy Dog thought it was a fair comment and fell asleep. However, he was immediately awakened. The Crazy Rooster was whispering right into his ear:

"What do I do? You must help me."

The Lazy Dog lazily opened one eye and looked right into the face of the disguised rooster, and said in a sleepy voice:

"Ahhh, must this and must that - - I don't think that I have to do anything,"

"Yes, yes, and yes, with an extra 'yes.' You must -
you MUST!"

The Crazy Rooster whispered desperately.

"I really don't know what to do!"

"It's probably not so much about what you should
do now, but what you should have done before.."

Exclaimed the now fully awake but still Lazy Dog,
and continued:

"You must put your claw down and resist."

"Resistance? But, I don't want to be unfriendly
with anyone,"

stammered The Crazy Rooster.

"You got to be true to yourself. You can't please
everyone anyway, so follow your own heart."

"Uh, okay, but how do I do that???"

The Lazy Dog shook his head in resignation.

The good atmosphere at Villa Viva
became more and more pleasant. Everyone found
a rhythm that pleased both themselves and the
community.Things were developing differently in
the henhouse. The first euphoric day was spent
celebrating the fact that no one could come in.
Everyone relaxed. Now they could live the dream
of not being subject to a master, or rather, a
mistress. They enjoyed their freedom.

But already on the second day, a sense of unease
began to spread. It started with one or two asking
what freedom was worth if they couldn't go out
of the henhouse. This prompted The Most Giant
Democratic Roosister to introduce Love Breaks,
a time when one could sit alone and contemplate
whether one preferred the warmth of the
community or the coldness of the outside world.

By the third day, it was clear that the model was
not well thought through. It was getting dirtier

because, well - the Angry Wife used to clean. Worse, they ran out of food. Because ... well - The Angry Wife used to feed them. The Most Giant Democratic Roosister realized that something had to be done, or else there would be a rebellion. But what?

On the night of the fourth day, she got up and sneaked over to the far corner of the hen house. Here, she had a secret exit made. Those who made the exit for her were instructed to keep it to themselves. If they didn't, she personally promised to crush all the eggs they laid in the future. It had worked so far, but with the developments that were underway, she might not be able to contain the simmering unrest.

She slipped out of the henhouse. Only the moonlight gave an idea of where she was and where she was going. The first stop was to find The Cunning Fox. She knew he used to hide behind the tree with the bench. Maybe she could get him to steal some food. If she had to do it herself, she would need so much time away that she would be exposed. Another thing was that she didn't know how to steal things, and The Cunning Fox did. After that, she would ask The Lazy Dog to make an automated cleaning thing. Rumour had it that he was good at that sort of thing, even if he was lazy. She didn't know if it was true, but she had to take the chance.

But neither of them would help. They both had asked her:

"What is in it for me??"

She hadn't thought about that. But suggested that they could have eggs. Both of them showed interest, but they wouldn't do anything before they got their payment.

"Okay, that's better than nothing,"

She thought to herself, as she sneaked back into the hen house. No one had seen her. Everyone was still asleep. Although there was peace at the moment, she was well aware that it wouldn't be long before they all went mad due to the stench and hunger.

Along with the rising sun, The Most Giant
Democratic Roosister awakened her flock with a:

"Cluck morning, cluck and crow! To you
wonderful Democratic Roosisters, who will soon
show the world a better path to happiness."

Most woke up right away, not so much because
of the sound of her voice, but more because the
tone was new and different, almost loving and
understanding. Still, the reaction from most was
the same:

"What the cluck is happening to you? We sleep
and need to sleep for a long time!

They responded in a mixed and discontented
chorus.

"My dear beings, let us have a gentle and loving
talk in the first light of a new, wonderful day."

Now, most of them were awake. The tone that
came from the Most Giant Democratic
Roosisters's beak was sweet and unsettlingly

different. So they listened anxiously but attentively to her speech:

"Wouldn't it be so lovely, Cluck, to lay some beautiful eggs again, like in the good old Clucking days?"

The Giant Democratic Roosisters responded as if from one one beak:

"What are you clutching about? It was you who wrote our manifesto. Here, rule number 1 states that we will no longer succumb to unreasonable demands. We won't be forced to work, meaning lay eggs, anymore. It's the first phase of our liberation."

"It was indeed true,"

Thought The Most Giant Democratic Roosister but continued:

"Yeah, but now we don't lay eggs for the Angry Wife and her Muted Man. Now we only lay eggs for our own good."

They clucked in total confusion:

"Why is it necessary?"

The Most Giant Democratic Roosister couldn't answer directly. She had indeed promised them freedom. That they wouldn't have to work. That everything would be a paradise. Now they were just neck-deep in chicken droppings - without food. Something clever had to be done:

" Dear Fellow Democrats,"

she began solemnly:

"We are under attack. The others have initiated a campaign against us. They are envious. They see their world falling apart while we live in paradise."

She took a short pause to feel if the mood had changed. And it clearly had. Now, they sat there indignantly, nodding encouragingly.
The sense of community was restored, so she continued:

"I don't know how they did it. But they have managed to sneak dirt into our sacred halls. They have stolen our food, so we starve. I fear that there is one among us who has made it possible."

A murmur went through the flock, and everyone looked at each other. Who could it be?

She continued:

"Let's keep a close eye on the situation and put an end to this betrayal,"

" Yeeaahh,"

The flock joined in.

"Let's build, implement, and live this wonderful alternative."

"Yaaahheeaa, clutch clutch hooray!"

They all roared with enthusiasm.

"It just requires that you lay eggs. That's all I'm

asking of you."

And now everyone was on board with her idea, fearing being accused as the traitor. Because when the traitor was found, she would be thrown out of their loving community and into the coldness of the outside world. The Most Giant Democratic Roosister had made that very, very clear.

In the outside world, in Villa Viva's gardens, they had almost forgotten about the hens. Only the mysterious cries from the henhouse reminded them of the time when they were part of daily life.

The Angry Wife had become good friends with the Angry Neighbour Wives after visiting them more often. The Muted Man could be heard humming from his office. The Lazy Dog could relax and did what he liked best - sleeping all day long. The Stupid Goose had time to tell her stories without being interrupted. Even The Cunning Fox enjoyed these days. Not because stealing had become easy, as it actually hadn't. He just enjoyed that everyone was in a good mood.

But that there was still life in the henhouse, a couple of residents of Villa Viva noticed the same night.

Shortly before midnight, the Most Giant Democratic Roosister paid a visit to The Lazy Dog. She first whispered very gently to wake him up. But he continued sleeping. Then she touched his nose. But nothing happened. She nudged his ear, pushed him, and pushed a little harder. Finally, she kicked him while exclaiming in annoyance:

"Wow, you sure sleep CLUCK soundly."
As he still hadn't moved, she shouted in suppressed rage:

"How can you have the audacity to act like I'm invisible?"

Afterward, she took a run-up and kicked The Lazy Dog in the head with her heavy military boot. The head turned all the way around with a rattling sound. Startled by the noise and the fact that the head had turned all the way around,

she hurried to the side of the doghouse to hide. What if someone had heard her, or him? But everything was completely silent in the darkness. She couldn't recall if she had heard his breathing before she kicked. But now it was entirely quiet. What if she had seriously harmed him? What if she had killed him? The Most Giant Democratic Roosister hurried past the big tree, hoping that she could at least convince The Cunning Fox. But he just responded:

"He he he, do you really think I would work for such a measly pair of eggs?"

She could somewhat agree with him. It wasn't much she had to offer from her flock. The fox was nearly dying of laughter. No matter what she tried, she couldn't convince him. She slunk back with no result. Just before she reached home, a voice behind her said:

"I saw it all."

Nearly jumping out of her feathers, she turned, turned around, and stared right into the beak of

The Crazy Rooster.

"I've seen you go in and out of the henhouse. I've seen you with the Lazy Dog. What were your intentions, may I ask"

Before she had a chance to answer, he continued:

"I've also seen you with the Cunning Fox. I know everything."

The Most Giant Democratic Roosister thought painfully hard and fast. What should she do with that fool? Was The Crazy Rooster trying to blackmail her? She chose to try kindness, even though it was really exhausting:

"So, you've seen me. Well, that sounds clucking great. Is there something I can cluck for you? Anything to make those things you've seen disappear?"

She chirped so sweetly, as possible. Her smile on the other hand looked more like a a curdled lemon beak. The Crazy Rooster replied:

"Yes, well, I really want to be with you. Can't I come into the henhouse? I promise not to tell anyone. Yes, I do, can you, uh, I mean Cluck."

The Most Giant Democratic Roosister could sense his submission. This could turn out to be an opportunity:

"Ok, you can come in on one condition. You have to stay in the background, and you have to try much harder to look like a hen."

The Crazy Rooster was about to jump in the air with joy. He eagerly followed The Most Giant Democratic Roosister into the darkness of the henhouse. Soon, he was sleeping in the farthest and least comfortable corner. But he didn't care, as long as he could be part of the flock.

The Most Giant Democratic Roosister, on the other hand, had a hard time sleeping. What if she had killed the dog?

The next day, she told the flock how everyone else in Villa Viva had betrayed them:

"And not only that, they have stolen the eggs you laid. Right in front of my eyes while I negotiated with them."

She could have kicked herself. No one should be able to get out or in. This hadn't been thoroughly thought through. The unrest had also spread like wildfire. The Giant Democratic Roosister's were on the verge of boiling over. But just before it happened, The Most Gigant Democratic Roosister regained her composure:

"I have figured out how the traitor has been getting in and out. Because I followed her. In doing so, I couldn't help but encounter the others in Villa Viva's Garden. I told them bluntly that if they don't immediately stop stealing our food, and especially stop filling our sacred house with filth, there will be consequences."

This quelled the anger among the hens. And after her next ploy, the mood shifted from being against her to being with her.

"And more important, now I know who the

traitor is."

" Who is it? Who?"

rippled through the crowd.

"I believe that the person probably knows it herself. It will be revealed in due time. Because of the betrayal, I must,"

she held a self-important pause, allowing everyone time to look sceptically at each other. Afterward, she continued:

"Yes, it's my task. My duty. Almost my destiny, to get our plan back on track. And the only way is to put an end to the madness of the others. Tomorrow, I will summon Villa Viva for a friendly conversation."

The rest of the day she sat and stared out the window. The dog was still lying as she had left him. Was he dead? It was definitely not good. She wondered when any of the others would realise something was seriously wrong.

The sound of nails being pulled out of wood met the residents of Villa Viva the next morning. The sun had just risen. Normally, the dog would have lifted his head a bit annoyed. But, as The Most Gigant Democratic Roosister had feared, nothing happened. The only thing that occurred on this quiet morning was that the door to the hen house now was open, and all the Hens marched out onto the courtyard in a long line. They had planned it so that they were ready in straight rows when The Angry Wife came out of the kitchen. And indeed, just as they had formed their parade, the Angry Wife emerged from the door. The Stupid Goose came out of her gate, which no one really ever remembered to close. The Cunning Fox happened to be there. The Muted Man rumbled in the kitchen, soon he would also emerge, to head to work. When The Most Giant Roosister spoke up:

"All you outsiders have driven it too far, but now it must...cluck, uh I mean, stop. We can no longer tolerate your way of,"

The Angry Wife interrupted her:

"of what??? What have the rest of us in Villa Viva done? It seems like it was you who wanted to live differently."

A sigh of despair went through the parading flock. Was there another explanation? The Most Giant Democratic Roosister pulled herself together and said angrily:

"We're tired of your lies. And not only that, you've placed a traitor among us. A traitor who has stolen our food and has sneaked dirt into our delightful sacred henhouse."

"We've done WHAT???"

The Angry Wife began but was interrupted:

"Yes, that's exactly what you have. And the traitor is right there."

The Most Giant Democratic Roosister pointed at The Crazy Rooster. Everyone looked astonished at him as he stood there with white feathers tied to his body. She continued:

"Was he perhaps one of the chosen ones? No, right? Yet, he entered the henhouse last night. He's the only one who has come and gone as he pleased. Or more accurately, as it pleased you."

She pointed at the Angry Wife:

"It's clear that cluck - cluck uh - you and The Crazy Rooster, well, all of you to be precise, are against us. You're envious. Therefore, our agreement must be clucked, uh, I mean, renegotiated."

"What agreement?

"We never entered into any agreement. It was you who kept us out, occupied the henhouse. And now you have the audacity to..."

The Most Giant Democratic Roosister interrupted The Angry Wife before she exploded in rage. With a condescending and authoritative voice, she continued:

"However you choose to look at it, we're simply

DDR

done with your oppression of minorities. Hmmm us hens. So, we demand more security. This means expanding the henhouse to our 6-meter safety zone. There, we'll build a new fence and establish a new 7-meter safety zone. And..."

Now it was The Most Giant Democratic Roosister who was interrupted by The Angry Wife's scornful laughter:

"Haha, why in the garden's weeds and flies' name would I ever agree to your ridiculous demands?"

The Most Giant Democratic Roosister tried to explain that the garden couldn't do without a henhouse and chickens who are doing....

"Doing what?"

The Angry Wife replied and continued:

"You don't lay eggs for us anymore. We've just learned to live without you. So, as far as I'm concerned, you can move somewhere else. I get eggs every day, just not from you. In fact, it's become cheaper and much more enjoyable.”

”What the CLUCK are you implying?”

It bursted from the hen, causing her fancy cap to spin around on her head. They were both so mad now that everyone stood stunned, following their quarrel, which kept reaching new heights with fresh accusations and profanities. The Cunning Fox took the opportunity to ask The Stupid Goose:

“What is a minorityngely?”

”It simply means being a smaller part of a community - so a minority. It is the opposite of a majority which means to be the largest part of a community”

The Cunning Fox thought for a moment and exclaimed a bit confused:

”So they believe they are a minority, even though they are the biggest group here in the garden. Mysterious, very very mysterious...”

The Most Giant Democratic Roosister stopped in
the middle of her furious monologue and shouted
into the face of the Angry Wife:

"BUT YOU'RE DEAD!!!"

"What, ME?"

The Angry Wife shouted back.

"No, no. L L Loo Look there..."

Everyone looked in the direction she was
pointing. There stood the Lazy Dog. Unleashed.
Everyone slowly stepped backward until they
were inside bushes or with their backs against the
house wall. The Lazy Dog stood with a piece of
paper. It was a speech he had prepared. He had
plenty of time to do so, since the evening he saw
The Most Giant Democratic Roosister kicking his
Lazy Dog teddy. He had just thought to give her
a little scare. He hadn't quite anticipated that
everyone else would be scared as well. He pulled
himself together and began his speech:

"Friends, please listen. There should be room for everyone because we are..."

But no one listened. They were all paralyzed with fear. Perhaps except for The Stupid Goose, who knew him better than most, and The Cunning Fox, who suddenly got busy helping The Most Giant Democratic Roosister, who had fainted in his arms.

The Lazy Dog gave up on his prepared speech and instead said something they all wanted to hear. While taking the Angry and very frightened Wife by the hand, he said:

"Come on, we had better make sure to get me back on the leash."

Everyone nodded, and the Angry Wife followed hesitantly. He helped her get the leash secured again. When the lock clicked, she jumped backward with a shout of joy:

"I have, yes I have. It's me. Who has. YES. Got the dog back on the leash. HURRAY!"

And everyone else cheered too, hugging each other. The Angry Wife became the hero of the day. Everyone forgot all about safety zones, and a spontaneous celebration broke out, lasting well into the night.

The Lazy Dog was following the festivities from his doghouse. There was just one mystery left. Why had his The Lazy Dog teddy emitted a groan? That, even he couldn't answer.

"Fortunately, it doesn't matter now."

He thought and fell asleep. The next day, Villa Viva returned to delightful uncontrolled and good old-fashioned chaos, and everyone got back into their usual roles.

The Fable of

The Wolf
beneath
the Star

"**H**ave you observed anything yet?"

Was written on the Lazy Dog's mobile screen.He quickly wrote back:

" Hmmmm, not yet,"

and focused even more sharply as he peered into his telescope. There were millions of tiny twinkling dots. He convinced himself that he could recognize each of them from the numerous star charts spread out on the large table in his basement library. A beep came, and yet another message:

"Exactly what I feared. You couldn't find a meat bone in a butcher shop."

" You have nothing to fear. I'll probably find something. Just give me a chance - I've only just set up the telescope."

It was late at night, and everyone in the neighbourhood was asleep. The moon was full, casting a strong light in the sky. The Lazy Dog stood at the top of the hill between all the houses. It was the first evening the new telescope, which he had been building for a long time, would face the test. All the Lazy Dogs in the little sleepy village, had been very intrigued by the universe lately, with all its stars, planets, and galaxies. They had studied the history together from Galileo to Einstein.

The Stupid Goose had just overheard them casually talking about Albert Einstein, and promptly she had one of his quotes ready:

"If people are good only because they fear punishment and hope for reward, then we are a sorry lot indeed."

The Lazy Dog just stared blankly at The Stupid Goose, trying to act as if nothing was happening, fearing to reveal anything. The plans were advanced, and there was no room for disruptions. The Lazy Dog and the Lazy Neighbour Dogs were quite certain that they themselves would have a place in history. They believed that they would be able to make special and groundbreaking scientific discoveries. That's why they had formed the TLDTLNAC, which was the abbreviation for The Lazy Dog and The Lazy Neighbour Dogs' Astronomy Club. They had met so often in the Lazy Dog's library, that his refrigerator was almost empty, of the meat bones he had been given. Bones he in fact didn't really like himself. So when the others arrived through the secret underground tunnels from the various gardens, he could offer them the treats that were visible in the light behind the refrigerator's glass door.

A ringtone had cut through the night and nearly caused The Lazy Dog to roll down the hill. He answered the phone and was met by a loud whispering voice:

"What about now?"

He looked up from the telescope and replied angrily:

"What on seven thousand million puppy's shit are you up to? Didn't we agree that we would only text each other?"

"Yeah okay, but have you seen anything now? - Have you?"

"No, I haven't. Now please..."

The Lazy Dog stopped in the middle of the sentence. And continued hesitantly:

"Um... a star?"

"What? Me?"

Came the uncertain voice from The Lazy Neighbour Dog.

"No, no, the sky."

"Am I the sky??? Now I think you've lost it. I asked if you've seen anything. So have you?"

The Lazy Dog was bursting with excitement:

"No, no, I mean, I think I've seen a star in the

Hallo

sky. There's a star in the sky."

The Lazy Neighbour Dog answered in a
slow and condescending tone:

"Yes, we know there are billions of stars in the
sky. Isn't that what we've studying in your
library?"

"YES YES, but this one is YO YES YO YOOOOOO,
this one is YIPPEEE YOOOUHOOO completely
new,"

shouted the Lazy Dog in pure excitement. And
continued whispering, as if his whisper could
erase his shout:

"I've seen a completely new star. I'm pretty sure
about it. I'm recording it now so that we can
study it tomorrow."

The voice from the phone answered a bit
annoyingly:

"okay okay it sounds all good. But the howl

you let out just before didn't sound very good, though. It's still ringing in my ear. I'm afraid you've awakened the whole neighborhood. If we get caught, it's all over."

"Don't worry, you have nothing to fear. Everyone is sleeping soundly; no one heard anything."

Assured the Lazy Dog. But he wasn't quite right about that.

All the Dominant Hens were sleeping soundly, except for The Most Dominant Hen. She often stayed awake at night because things weren't as she desired. Everything just went on its merry and chaotic way. There was nothing she could use to install the necessary fear. She was afraid she may never gain power. Just as she had finished that thought, a howl echoed in the night. She looked out the window, and despite having white feathers, she turned even paler - chalk-white she screamed:

"UUUUUUUUH UUUUUUUHOOOOHWOLF WOLF WOLF."

The other Dominant Hens awoke with a jolt and saw to their horror the chalk white silhouette of the Most Dominant Hen in the window.

"GHOOOOOSTTTT"

They yelled out in unison, fainted, and a bunch of their feathers, rose in a white cloud around them. The Crazy Rooster wasn't as frightened, but to show loyalty, he cut the strings holding the white feathers around him. Then he tossed them in the air and pretended to faint.

The Most Dominant Hen turned around and looked squinted into the cloud of feathers:

"But for Cluck sake, what the feather is going on? There's a WOLF out there."

"What, um where, um how? There was a ghost, I saw it with my own eyes,"

one of the Dominant Hens accidentally said. The Most Dominant Hen grabbed her by the scruff of the neck and dragged her to the window. At the same time, most of the other Dominant Hens were regaining their composure. What they feared more than a ghost was precisely a wolf. And there, in front of the moon, stood a:

"WOOOOOLF,"

blurted out of the beak of The Dominant Hen, who was dangling in the grip of The Most Dominant Hen. Most of them fainted again. The Crazy Rooster stayed lying down just to be safe and cautiously watched through a half-open eye. It was particularly important here to follow the flock to avoid getting into trouble.

The wolf disappeared. The moon went down. The sun rose. The Dominant Hens began to pull them self together. Some laid back on the eggs with ruffled feathers. Others picked up their feathers from the floor and tried to put them back in place. In fact, the Crazy Rooster was the first to get his plumage in order, with strings that secured the fine white chicken feathers to his body. It was important that none of The

Dominated Hens were reminded that he wasn't a she, or whatever it was.

There was almost calm again in the small hen house. But only almost. The Most Dominant Hen was busy. Here was finally a fear that could be fueled. While the others fussed with their feathers and eggs, The Most Dominant Hen walked around the neighbor gardens spreading the story of the wolf on the hill.

Before The Angry Wife and The Angry Neighbour Wives came out to collect their eggs, the gardens were in chaos. It was unmistakable that something was very wrong. Soon, even The Angry Wives and their Muted Men understood that fear had arrived in the little sleepy town. Over hedge and fence, people were heard saying:

"Imagine a wolf."

"Yes, have you heard that it has already killed several animals in the forest?"

"No - you're not serious?"

Yes, it was true, for that was precisely what

everyone had been telling each other. However, no one had seen anything - yet. A topic that, despite everything, preoccupied The Muted Men. They would like some evidence of the mischief the wolf had made because they were well aware of the direction everything was taking. A path they rightly feared.

"What do you think they'll come up with now?"

"Yes, it smells like more work for us."

" Just wait, soon it's probably going to be our fault."

And sure enough, their fears were justified. Soon, The Angry Wives believed that this would never have happened if their Muted Men hadn't been so much at work. Too little at work. Too little in the garden. Taking too long to leave the house. Not doing the dishes. Earning too little. Being too much with friends. Saying too much. Yes, everything they had done or not done was now to blame for this misfortune.

" If there actually IS a wolf?"

one of The Muted Men had said accidentally.
After which none of them dared to attempt
alternative explanations to the plain truth - at
least according to The Angry Wife and The Angry
Neighbour Wives.

That's why not everyone slept in the little sleepy
town that night. While chickens, foxes, and dogs
got a good night's sleep, The Muted Men were
assigned to keep watch and look out for the wolf.
All night they walked around in pairs with their
pitchforks or other tools serving as kind of
weapons.

Now, it's not entirely true that all the dogs were
asleep either. The Lazy Dog paced up and down
the floor in his library, fuming. He certainly
couldn't sleep. How was he supposed to keep an
eye on the new exciting star, that was emerging
in the sky? In fact, there weren't many of the Lazy
Neighbor Dogs who got any sleep either.
After they had reveiwed the footage, it became
clear that this celestial phenomenon they had

discovered could be entirely new. And now they couldn't go out to study it because of all the foolish people running around.

The Most Dominant Hen, on the other hand, was delighted. That is - outwardly, she made an effort to appear horrified. But inside, she was bubbling with joy. It was good to see that fear was spreading. With fear, it was easier to convince, first and foremost, The Angry Wives, that changes had to happen. And to her delight, she saw that she didn't even have to do anything. The Muted Men were already working to create a new and lovely orderly atmosphere. An order that would bring security. By "orderly," The Most Dominant Hen meant less freedom, and by "secure" she meant submissiveness - two things she loved more than anything else. So changes based on fear and submission came naturally.

The reduced freedom was especially noticeable at night. Even though The Muted Men were outdoors, it was with plans laid out by the Angry Wives. Guard schedules and specific routes to follow were implemented. The entire area was

soon covered by the patrolling of The Muted
Men. Despite that, no one had yet seen any wolf,
but it certainly didn't stop the talk, quite the
opposite. Whispers started behind hedges and
closed doors. But as time passed, this
reality became more and more accepted. So even
though no one had directly seen anything, doubt
that it was out there faded. There were
eyewitness accounts, however, never from the
direct source. Someone had heard from someone
who had heard it at the football club, where there
was someone who knew someone who had
definitely encountered the wolf - bang in the
middle of the street. They had barely made it
indoors. There was no doubt. The wolf was real.

The Lazy Dog couldn't help but hear all the
chatter coming from all sides while he lay
pretending to sleep in his chain. He was about to
explode. There was no wolf. It was him they had
seen. Imagine how stupid they could be. Even
though he had made a big noise, he didn't
resemble a wolf in any way.

" How do we get control of that star?"

he said to himself, thinking he was alone. Unfortunately, he wasn't.

"Control?? Over a star??"

asked The Stupid Goose and The Cunning Fox simultaneously. They had come by coincidentally without The Lazy Dog noticing. He looked up startled and was well aware, that he had already said too much, but tried with:

"Uh, um, you see, I was just thinking about something or someone or..."

He was interrupted.

"What's the star you want to get control of?"

they both wanted to know. The Lazy Dog felt he was exposed. If he was, it would be the end of libraries, stargazing, and all the other things he loved.

"Are you trying to attach a remote control to a star?"

The Cunning Fox wanted to know and started laughing. The Stupid Goose added:

And once the control is on, how remote do you want to go?"

The Lazy Dog breathed a sigh of relief. Maybe they hadn't figured it out. But then The Stupid Goose said:

"You might want to go as remote as up that hill? And check on the star?"

The Lazy Dog replied in dispear:

"Uh, no. Why would I do that? And how could I even get up there? You can see that I'm chained up."

" Yeah, yeah, right. I just heard rumors from some of the other Lazy Neighbor Dogs."

said The Stupid Goose.

Now fear really began to take hold of The Lazy

Dog. What had they heard? And why couldn't the Other Lazy Neighbour Dogs just be - well, lazy enough to keep quiet. He continued:

"What I was trying to say was..."

he began hesitantly, searching for a story that was credible enough.

" ...that The Angry Wife is a star here in Villa Viva, and..."

The two looked at him suspiciously.

"The Angry Wife? - I didn't really think you were on the same wavelength as her,"

The Cunning Fox blurted out.

"Nah, hmm, hu, one might well think. But umm, you see. Hmmm, she's sort of a star here in umm, the garden. Or at least she thinks she is, and... she... um..."

He wove and searched for the words but was

pleased to see that the two accepted the fact that she thought she was a star. Now it was just a matter of moving on with the lie. There was a bit of truth, that he was in the process of telling a lie. It was certainly not something he liked. Lying was very bad, he thought. But the truth would be much worse. He chuckled inwardly at this comical paradox. Maybe it could even be fun to get rid of this fear. He straightened up:

”And even though she’s hard to control, it would be quite good if it could be done,”

Somewhat more determined and serious The Stupid Goose continued:

”Yeah, but what I’ve heard from the other gardens is that all you Lazy Dogs are on the hunt for a real star. A brand new one in the sky.”

If only The Stupid Goose could stop sticking her beak into everything, thought The Lazy Dog irritably. And once again, he feared that he couldn’t avoid being exposed. Something else had to be done.

"Who the heck saying such nonsense?"

he continued, hoping to expose The Lazy
Neighbour Dog who was to blame for this mess.
Because then he could have a reckoning with
him. But The Stupid Goose kept her beak shut, so
he had to continue elaborating. Even though he
really felt that it was wrong.

"I mean, have you ever heard of a dog being
interested in the night sky?"

The Stupid Goose had to admit that she had
never heard of it. But then again:

"what about the space dog, Laika?"

The Lazy Dog took over:

"Listen to you ramble on. You sound like you are
in outer space yourself. Admittedly one of the
first living beings in space was a dog. But it's not
like it chose that. Or wanted to go. I don't think it
even understood what was happening."

”Okay, okay, we can agree on that, The Angry
Wife behaves as if she's a star!”

said The Stupid Goose and looked questioningly
at The Cunning Fox. He nodded, not feeling very
cunning, but continued:

”Yes, that's right. And someone should really get
to grips with this. Every day, there are new rules
about what we can and cannot do. All because of
a wolf no-one has seen.”

That was more true than any of them could know,
pondered The Lazy Dog. The conversation was
heading in the right direction. It just needed a
decisive conclusion.

”Lies won't help us,”

The Lazy Dog looked seriously. He felt like he
was winning and was on top now, so he
continued:

”We have to stick to what we know.”

"This might be true,"

replied The Stupid Goose, to The Lazy Dog's displeasure. This conversation needed to end here and she was still talking!

"You see, there can be cases where lies can actually save the situation,"

The Stupid Goose continued:

"Winston Churchill, the English Prime Minister during World War II, once said: In wartime, the truth is so valuable that it must always be protected by a wall of lies."

And so ended this somewhat peculiar conversation. The Lazy Dog was almost satisfied. It didn't end badly, but he wondered if it ended well. The quote from the Stupid Goose lingered in his mind. What did it really mean? Was there truly a truth that was best kept behind a protective wall of lies? He didn't like the thought. But during the night, the idea crept into his head that maybe there was a way to act on this, a way that could solve the whole detestable affair. So he could return and studying the new star—in peace.

It was difficult to hide the black circles under his. The Muted Man looked in the rearview mirror of his car. Yes, they were still black. Of course it had been a long day at the office. But he hadn't had much sleep either. His Angry Wife and all The Angry Neighbour Wives were busy changing watch schedules, expanding the area where they were looking for the wolf. It was soon their ideas he feared more than the wolf itself.

"If there was a wolf?"

he thought and became afraid that the Angry Wives could read his thoughts. Doubting whether there was a wolf was strictly forbidden. Because there just was. In fact, most of The Angry Wives believed they had seen it themselves. That was at least what was discussed when they all met for tea, yoga, invited expert speakers, or other entertainment to pass the evenings. Even the famous Really Good Nurse had been there with good advice. All while their Muted Men followed the wives' predetermined routes and rules in the cold evening darkness. In fact, the tradition of meeting at each other's homes, now that they were all alone, had become a welcome and delightful change. The Angry Wives enjoyed it to the fullest.

The Muted Man raged inside as much as he dared. Until his mobile phone pulled him out of his thoughts with a loud, piercing guitar solo ringtone sound that he had made himself. He fumbled to pick up the phone.

"oh, who is this, it's me speaking? Hello?,"

he said, slightly confused. He hadn't expected any calls today. In fact, no one other than his wife ever called him, and that was to the ringtone of Jaws.

"Heylloooo,"

He said once more, because the only thing he could hear was someone wheezing in the background. He listened in silence for as long as he dared. And just as he decided to hang up, a deep voice said:

"I am the Wolf. I am the one you are looking for." The voice sounded somewhat distorted:

"Are you on your way home in your mini-golf?"

the voice continued. The Lazy Dog could have bitten his tongue. It had just slipped out of him because The Angry Wife always referred to The Muted Man's Polo as Mini Golf. She so desperately wanted him to upgrade to the somewhat more expensive version called a Golf.

The Lazy Dog sat down in his basement, in front of a microphone he had invented, that made him sound like a wolf with a human voice.

"Mini Golf - for goodness' sake, you tame dog poop. This could expose me before I've even started my plan,"

The Lazy Dog spluttered angrily into for himself. He covered the microphone so that The Muted Man wouldn't hear. However, The Muted Man didn't have time to hear anything at all. He was stunned by what he had already heard. So he didn't pay attention anyway. He just said slowly and almost hesitantly, as if he weren't quite awake:

"Woooolfff"

"YES YES THE WOLF OR MAYBE MORE CORRECT-WOLFCHICKEN"

Exclaimed the Lazy Dog a bit irritated.

"Wolf-Chicken?"

The Muted Man was now more attentive.

"Absolutely accurate - yes. I am the wolf you think you've seen. But in reality, I'm not a wolf at all. I just look like a wolf, but I am the Holy-Wolf-Chicken, the god that all chickens worship, including yours",

The Muted Man had fallen completely silent. However, he finally managed to wrest a few cautious words from his mouth.

"W-Why. Why are you calling me?"

"Well, you see, I have chosen your village. Not just here on Earth, where you live, but among all the planets in the universe."

The Lazy Dog had learned from his lie to The Stupid Goose and The Cunning Fox that if a lie was to be believed, then it had better be a big one.

"I have traveled among the stars for a very long time to find the perfect place to lay my Divine Golden Egg. It only happens once in my lifetime, so the location must not only be perfect, it must adhere to some special rules,"

The Lazy dog ellaborated

"Rules?"

Said The Muted Man, more to reassure himself.
Here was a word he could understand.

"Yes, rules are necessary. That's what my wife
says too."

He said with relief in his voice. The Lazy Dog
had to go outside the soundproof room and close
the door gently behind him to let out a burst of
laughter. He tiptoed back to the microphone and
continued:

"Uh, yes, indeed, it's good that she uh agrees with
me. The rules are that the egg must be laid near
a very beautiful hen house. The behavior of the
chickens must be exemplary. Pretty and
obedient. They must be skilled at laying eggs.
The last preferably to an extreme degree, which I
have observed from my spaceship that yours are."

"Golden egg? - Divine?"

The Muted Man was starting to wake up. What a
charming Wolf, uh, Wolf-uh-Chicken, who had,
uh, traveled through, uh, space. A small voice

inside his head tried to warn him. Something might be wrong here. But The Muted Man dismissed the voice and lapped up all the praise and flattery. And said:

"What is this? This special Divine Golden Egg?"

"My Divine Golden Egg - ha he hmmmph,"

The Lazy Dog had to once again muffle the microphone to get control over a suppressed laughter.

"So, ha mmmpfr, I'd say. Yes - it has some special properties for the finder. The Divine Golden Egg indeed grants infinite knowledge, irresistible insight, unprovable wisdom, and immeasurable wealth."

The Muted Man was all ears now.

"Immeasurable wealth? I wonder how much more that is than incredible."

The Lazy Dog continued with his distorted voice:

"I just can't have peace to lay my Divine Golden
Egg. As long as you Muted Men roam around
at night. If you want a special chance to get the
golden egg that will change your life, so you don't
have to slave away at your office in the city, then
you must help me."

The Muted Man didn't hear the honks from the
other cars in the queue. His car stood completely
still, while he was listening intently to the Lazy
Dog's distorted speech. Could this really be true?
Was this happening to him? The silence on the
other end of the phone told The Lazy Dog that he
had caught him. Now, it was just a matter of
making the lie so far fetched to be believable.

"First and foremost, give me peace at night.
Next, choose a secret place where you can build a
divine nest for me and my golden egg."

The Lazy Dog hesitated for a moment as he
invented the rest of the requirements:

"And, uh, yes - you see - you must convince the
other Muted Men that the wolf hunt should take

place on the other side of the forest. Uh, and that it's best in the afternoon, uh, because, uh, the wolf, uh…"

"…is not a wolf at all."

Came the proud response from The Muted Man.

"What ever, the only thing that matters is that no-one must know anything about who I really am. It can only be you. Otherwise, it's all ruined. I won't lay any devine gold egg. You won't become much more than stinking, or maybe even outright rude rich. You won't get a wife who is sweet instead of angry. And all that sort of thing,"

he hurried to say, with so much conviction in his voice, that The Muted Man wouldn't tell anything to any one.

"How about my wife. Am I not allowed to tell her either?"

The Muted Man was on the verge of tears. Finally, he had a story that would make her

proud of him. And yet, he couldn't say anything.
He had been silent his entire life. But now, he
had something that he needed to tell her

"Yes, yes, of course,"

The Lazy Dog hadn't thought about that. But
maybe it wasn't such a bad idea after all. That
way, they would keep each other in check.

"She's supposed to help you. You should be a
team."

The Muted Man was slowly regaining his
composure and asked a bit skeptically, but
mostly in wonder.

"How am I supposed to convince the other Muted
Neighbour Men that the wolf should only be
hunted during the day?"

"Because, um, the wolf, um...?"

Why shouldn't they hunt the wolf at night?
Well well, that was a pretty good question

- he had to take a chance:

"Because in the afternoon, the wolf sleeps and is easy to catch. It's the night they should fear - that's when it's most dangerous."

The Muted Man sat nodding, as it sounded logical enough. That was something he could handle.

"But why on the other side of the forest?"

He said almost in a whisper, as he was afraid of annoying The Holy Wolf-Chicken. To his relief, he responded politely and kindly:

"You don't need to worry. The others will accept it all. Remember, I am kind of a god. So most things go according to my will."

"Oh, yes, um, of course."

The Muted Man stammered out and thought to himself:

"How foolish can I allow myself to be?"

but he actually already knew the answer. His Angry Wife had told him a thousand times.

The Muted Man's thoughts were interrupted. By the distorted voice of the Lazy Dog:

"Remember you are the chosen one. The special one. The only one,"

with those words in his ears, The Muted Man remained as silent as he had never been in his life. He almost dared not to breathe. He had to grasp every word. Was he truly chosen for this special task?

The Lazy Dog hung up and let out a rolling chuckle. He then called the next Muted Man. Soon, all the men in the village felt that they were the special chosen one. The Lazy Dog sat back, amazed. It was apparently unbelievably easy to make people believe, as long as it was something they didn't quite understood, wrapped in a story that was far-fetched enough. The Lazy Dog noted

MIC

it down in his big black notebook:

"This is knowledge worth fearing if it falls into
the wrong hands."

That night, no-one was out searching. the
hushed whispering from all the houses, was the
only thing revealing life in the small town. The
men made plans with their Angry Wives.
The next day, The Muted Man talked to all the
other Muted Men. The first part of the plan was,
after all, to convince everyone to move the hunt
to the other side of the forest and only in the
afternoon. He had feared the task; what if they
didn't do as he said?

But all The Muted Men thought the same that
evening, that it had almost been too easy. They
feared that someone might have overheard their
secret and blabbed.

Therefore, the somewhat peculiar situation arose
in the days that followed, where they were afraid
to talk to each other. If they did, they were not
really daring to say anything - conversations

might sound like:

"Hi, um, how are you?"

"Well, I'd rather hear how you're doing?"

"Now I think it was me who asked first?"

"I'm not quite sure about that,"

and when they finally ended the conversation,
you could hear the others in the gardens saying:

"After you."

"No, you please. I asked first..."

In fear of losing their status as the only chosen
ones with the prospect of filthy richness and all
that, their conversations dwindled. It became
quiet in the small village. Everyone kept to
themselves, or rather, attended to their sacred
wolf nests.

The Lazy Dog kept an eye on the developments. It

was progressing too slowly because even though they had started guarding in the
afternoon, everyone knew there wasn't a wolf. So, they came up with all sorts of sick excuses not to show up. Instead, they spent the nights building on their Wolf Chicken Nests. Therefore, The Lazy Dog still couldn't get out looking for the star. Something more efficient was needed to be done.

The Lazy Dogs held meetings night after night while their Lazy Dog teddy-bears were chained up in their doghouses. They were so absorbed in finding a solution that several Lazy Dogs forgot about their teddy bear substitutes.

In this way, many of The Angry Wives and The Muted Men could have seen two dogs at the same time in the doghouses. But they were so preoccupied with the Divine Golden Egg that they didn't notice anything at all.

"This is the most peculiar thing I've ever encountered,"

The Lazy Dog shouted across the large table in the library. He looked seriously at all the other Lazy Dogs:

"Even though it's tempting to take action, it seems that the most effective thing we can do at this point, is to do nothing. We must patiently wait until they realize that nothing is happening."

"Unless we can help it along,"

One of The Lazy Neighbor Dog interrupted.

"Speak up, let's all hear"

The Lazy dog said.

"Well, you see, now when they all believe that they are the chosen one."

They all nodded.

"What if they found out that someone other than themselves had found the Divine Golden Egg?"

The Lazy Dog replied:

"They'll never fall for that. As you yourself say, each of them believes they are the only chosen one, and only them. No one else knows anything, except, of course, their Angry Wives."

"Exactly. Think about all the suspicion and fear that can arise in this situation. They might question if they were truly the only chosen one. They could fear that their wife has revealed their hiding spot, and someone else has stolen the egg. Or that it was all a hoax. The last would be the worst for them because who can they tell THAT to, or complain? Think about the shame. Think about the desperation."

The Lazy Dog looked over his yellow-tinted screen glasses. This wasn't actually a bad idea at all, and continued:

"Just so I understand you correctly. You want to start a rumor that the Divine Golden Egg has been found. It will surely come as a shock to all of them. How can that be possible? Who are they supposed to tell it to? And what would they even be able to say? It was a secret, which means none of them can really do anything. They will all be forced to suspect each other. Therefore, there's only one way out for them, and that is to get back into the old rhythm, as quickly as possible. They have to do everything they can to forget it all, deny it, and repress it. Play along and pretend they know nothing. Hmmm. It might work. If it does, it will get us out of this mess faster. But how can we make it happen?"

The Crazy Rooster became the key to spreading the rumor. He would do anything to prove that he was a worthy gossip-hen, and he wouldn't dare ask questions. Soon, all the henhouses knew that one of the neighbours had found the Divine Golden Egg. And it was such that once the chickens knew, well, then the Angry Wives knew. And when the Angry Wives knew, their Muted Men knew instantly.

An ominous and oppressive atmosphere quickly spread through the small sleeping town. For a while, allThe Angry Wives and The Muted Men

looked askance at each other. They all feared
what would happen when the one who had
obtained the Divine Golden Egg started using
their unfounded wisdom, and perhaps most of
all, their new filthy fortune.

But it went exactly as The Lazy Neighbour Dog
had predicted. As the days passed, and nothing
happened, everyone gradually began to settle
back into their familiar routines. The suspicion
was buried, but only just beneath the surface.
The Lazy Dogs prepared to venture out
under the starry sky once again. They retrieved
the telescope and readied their secret key. So
when the night fell, they could unlock
themselves and get out and see for themselves.
Was there really a new star on the way?
After much toil and trouble, they were ready.
But then the sky became covered with thick dark
clouds. The wind rose, causing the leaves to blow
off the autumn trees. With the wind came rain,
and with the rain came the storm. They all had
to seek shelter indoors before being blown away.
However, the telescope managed to take in quite
a bit of water.

VIL
VIVA

The storm grabbed hold of the small sleeping town and shook it thoroughly. The fine, large, rusty metal letters on the house gable, proudly displaying the house's name - Villa Viva - vibrated strongly throughout the night. So, the next morning, when the wind had subsided, and the sun once again broke through to the small sleeping town. Two of the letters had been blown down. Instead of Villa Viva, it now read "Vil Viva."

The Stupid Goose, was the only one who understood that it no longer said "The Living Village" but "The Malicious Life." She didn't have the heart to tell the others about the change. Now that the little house with its garden and all its inhabitants almost had returned to the uncontrolled and familiar chaos. Star-gazing came to a halt as the telescope had been spoiled by the storm. Everything seemed peaceful.

But for how long?

The **Villa Viva** books are dedicated
to the future, and for me it is
my grandchildren
Aksel and **Oskar Bo Appel**

And a special thanks to Jeanne Rungby.